I0547285

nickel plated gold

ALSO BY BRIAN BIEBER

Learn About What's Called Ghosts & Horses

Be Sympathy for Ghosts & Horses

Nickel Plated Gold

Stories

by
Brian Bieber

Ghosts & Horses
Sioux Falls, South Dakota

Nickel Plated Gold
Copyright © 2013 by Brian Bieber

Cover design by: Kiel Mutschelknaus
kielm.com

GhostsAndHorses.com

Printed in the United States of America
First Printing

For my dad, Myron Bieber.
I started writing because he likes to read.

For my mom, Mary Bieber.
I started making jokes because she likes to laugh.

NICKEL PLATED GOLD

FOREWORD

by
Dessa

A dozen years ago, while I was half drunk in his living room, Brian Bieber explained Fugazi to me. The crazy live show, the straight-edge lifestyle, the aversion to shirts, the unassailable punk credibility. Brian had seen footage of a concert where the lead singer performed a significant portion of the show hanging upside-down from a basketball hoop. Brian played me a few songs, hoping to convert me. No dice. At the time, I was listening to a lot of sad folk artists and (arguably sadder) indie rappers. He turned off the stereo, reached over the couch and picked up an unremarkable acoustic guitar. Slowly, he plucked out a few Fugazi melodies. That worked. Hearing the music in a more familiar timbre and at a more familiar tempo rendered it accessible to me. He set aside the guitar and we started listening again.

* * *

Since the day we met in college, Brian's always been an easy guy to root for. Even at the start of our careers, when a competitive spirit might have naturally emerged, it was impossible to muster any real jealousy when his work was selected for a publication we both admired. He was too diligent, too kind-spirited—you looked at Brian, and any competitive impulse became patently ridiculous and just sorted of clattered to the ground like silverware. Which was kind of a pain in the ass because I could have used a little antagonism. Can't pick your rivals, I guess.

Brian's a good writer for many of the same reasons he was a successful Fugazi ambassador. Without a lot of fanfare or exposition, he can connect what you don't know with what you do. He recognizes there are moments in art that should be beautiful. There are moments that should not. His swift pacing allows him to do humor successfully; his facility with tone allows him to do absurdism; but it's his rendering of human nature that defines some of my favorite Brian stories.

Reading one of the pieces in this collection, I thought to myself, "Oh my God, this isn't about me, is it?" I got choked up. Then I realized, chastising myself for my idiocy, that almost any reader could see themselves in that particular story. If Zsa Zsa Gabor happened to know Brian personally, she'd probably be just as sure it was written about her. That's why it's good.

If you're buying this copy of his book at a reading, do yourself a favor and have Brian sign it. Guy's going places. Do yourself a bigger favor and don't have him sign your name on it—this thing could be worth real money on eBay someday.

Dessa.

Author's note:

Most of these stories are completely made up, but some of them are partly true, and a couple of them are almost completely true. It's not really all that important which are which.

However, I do think it is important to note that whenever an actual, real person is mentioned by name in this book, that name is not the person's real name.

Author's note (2):

I'm pretty sure that, despite her concerns, none of the following pieces are about Dessa.

But maybe I'm wrong. I've been telling some of the stories in this collection for over a decade now, and even I sometimes forget what's what.

Several years after it was published on their website, the good folks at McSweeney's asked to include "Tales of Erotica" in their 2008 humor anthology. I was so used to the piece being a joke that, after the book was published, I was stunned to receive an email from an old friend containing a single line: "Am I Steven Seagal?"

I thought about lying, of course, but the lady in question has an excellent nose for bullshit. Luckily, she took the characterization in the spirit it was intended, and chose to be flattered instead of angry. (Hi, Melissa!)

I don't know which piece Dessa is referring to, and I don't plan to ask. I suppose I'd rather just let these stories be stories. And I'd rather you do the same.

...That said, if I had to put money on it, I'd bet she thinks she's the kangaroo on page 24.

Author's note (3)

While we're on the subject, I think it's also important to note that even though this book includes passages in which I speculate about how I would fight certain animals, no animals were hurt in the making of this book. Because I would never do anything to hurt an animal.

Author's note (4)

I guess it's possible that an animal could have somehow been hurt during the production phase of this book. It's not like I was on the assembly line supervising or anything. But I can't imagine a circumstance in which a printing press would find it necessary to harm an animal in the process of printing a book.

Author's note (5)

Still, if you hear anything about an animal being hurt in the making of my book, please give me a call:

605 323-9247

I'm not sure what I could do about it, but I would definitely take my business to a new printer, if I could find one with similarly competitive rates.

Please don't call after 10:00PM CST, unless it's a real emergency.

THE SYSTEM

I'm sorry," he told me, "but I don't think you have a case."

He was probably right, this lawyer. I nodded and leaned back in the comfortable chair. I tapped a finger on my knee. I leaned forward in the chair. "Are you sure?" I asked.

"Yes. Very."

This guy meant business. He was definitely the kind of guy you want to have on your team.

"Hmm," I said. "What would I need to do exactly— what would it *take*—for us to get this case into really solid shape?"

The lawyer looked me in the eye for a long time, which I liked, because it showed he was a straight shooter. He said, "I really don't think there's anything you can do. Honestly."

I leaned back in my comfortable chair. "Just a ballpark estimate...."

The lawyer was silent. It might have been a test.

"Just so you know," I told the lawyer. "I'm in this for the long haul. You don't have to worry about me getting cold feet."

I leaned back in my comfortable chair, and laced my fingers behind my head. "My feet are toasty, friend."

I winked at him.

The lawyer leaned forward in his comfortable chair. "I don't know how else to say it," he said. "You don't have a case. In the most literal way possible. I cannot represent you."

I nodded. I tapped my lip thoughtfully. I considered the manila evidence folder I brought with me. It was sitting between us on the lawyer's desk. It was empty.

"Can we go over the facts again?" I asked him, leaning forward in my comfortable chair.

He didn't respond.

"I think we need to come at this from a different angle," I continued. "I think the solution is right there in front of us, and we're just so damn close that we can't see it!"

I rapped my knuckle against the top of his desk to show my passion.

"I have another appointment," he said.

I imagined us in court, me in a suit—a nice suit, different from the one I have now—sitting at a table next to him. The courtroom is full. He is screaming at the judge: *My client is not the one on trial here!* I am calm, but not smug. I have complete confidence in him.

"Hmm," I said. He looked at me hard, eyes smoldering with some kind of emotion.

I reviewed the day's events: Woke up at noon. Masturbated in the shower. Ate a cup of yogurt. Arrived ten minutes late for this meeting with the lawyer.

Hmm.

I was going to have to trace my steps back further, to the beginning of all this…

I leaned forward in the chair. Put my elbow on my knee. Put my chin on my palm. I looked at the shelves of books on the wall of the lawyer's office. Most of them were nice leather-bound volumes. I didn't read the spines.

I took a deep breath. The lawyer sighed, and looked at his watch. For a while, that's how things stayed.

WHAT KIND OF
GHOST
DO YOU HAVE?

CLUMSY GHOST

You are mindful to keep delicate objects away from the edges of coffee tables and counter tops, lest they fall mysteriously to the floor. You hear strange, disembodied voices in the attic. They say, "whoops!"

You have a clumsy ghost.

Your home's previous owner died a tragic, but avoidable and seemingly far-fetched death.

"Why was this beautiful home so inexpensive?"

"The real estate agent said something about a loose floorboard, and a candelabra, and the previous owner's stereo not being grounded right."

This is a typical conversation in a house with a clumsy ghost.

SICK GHOST

Your husband is working the late shift. Your children are sound asleep in their bedrooms down the hall.

So where is that soft, spectral sniffling coming from?

You find yourself woken in the night by the sound of a phlegmy cough, followed by an embarrassed and spooky, "Excuse me."

You have a sick ghost.

You go through more Kleenex than seems possible for a mortal family of four. When you wake to find an entire bottle of Robitussin emptied overnight, you enroll your screw-up fourteen-year-old son in an outpatient chemical dependency treatment program. Only after you cart Brad off to a dull gray state hospital in a fit of exasperation—only to have the cough syrup disappearances continue—does it occur to you that the answer to this mystery might only be found beyond the grave... and under the weather.

GHOST WITH A GOOD SENSE OF HUMOR

You notice it first during a Buster Keaton feature on TCM: a faint, chilling giggle here, a soft, spine-tingling chuckle there. There is someone—or *something*—with you in your studio apartment. And it likes slapstick.

The spirit reveals its more sophisticated tastes as you read *Without Feathers* on the toilet. You feel a presence over your shoulder. At first you think you are being watched, and your blood runs cold. Then it begins to feel more like the presence is just reading along. You still feel uncomfortable.

Weeks later, you and your girlfriend are making out on the couch, pretending to watch *Dr. Strangelove*. As you begin to move your hand up her back, under her shirt, the mood is suddenly shattered by a supernatural guffaw coming from the other end of the sofa. She bites your lip in surprise. You look at each other for a moment, then at the other end of the sofa. Then you get back to kissing. Twenty minutes later, as you remove each other's clothing the same way you always do, it feels a little kinky.

TALL GHOST

You've heard of things that go "bump" in the night. This thing doesn't necessarily go "bump" just in the night, but it usually does so near a door frame. Then it goes, "ow."

The hallway floor is piled deep with thick, tasteful cream carpeting. One night, as you walk from the den to the bathroom, you hear the floorboards creak. You stop. The creaking stops. You continue to walk. The creaking resumes. You stop again, quickly, and so does the creaking, but not as quickly as you do. For a few moments the only sound in the hallway is the pounding of your pulse. Then, as you stand there, stock-still, the creaking begins again. You take a deep breath, and very slowly, you turn around. Advancing toward you is something invisible. It must be pretty heavy, because in the thick carpet it leaves the impressions of two larger-than-average human feet. Chillingly, they are proportionate to someone—or *something*—tall. The sight of the ample footprints sends you screaming from the house.

As you wait in the driveway for your parents to return from their monthly dinner out, you consider the basketball hoop hanging above the garage door, and you wonder if the poor, tormented soul haunting your home can dunk.

THE YEAR IN FILM: 1976

Editor's note: From 1968–1989, Brian Bieber wrote a weekly, nationally syndicated arts & entertainment newspaper column. The following piece appeared in 482 North American newspapers on Tuesday, December 28, 1976.

As my longtime readers know, I am a lover of great film. So you can only imagine how saddened I am by how few truly good films are produced every year by the money-grubbing fat cats in Hollywood.

These fat cats should be ashamed of themselves for releasing (i.e. crapping) so much crap into our movie theaters. That is why, since 1968, I have made it an annual tradition to end the year by publicly shaming them for doing so.

And so, without further ado, it is my "pleasure" to present the Top 5 Worst Films of 1976:

5. ALL THE PRESIDENT'S MEN

Adapted from the 1974 non-fiction book of the same name, this snoozefest sleepily recounts the tedious events of the Watergate break-in, which nobody cares about anymore, because it happened over six years ago! Memo to the fat cats in Hollywood: The reason we go to movies is because we like things that are made up, and we don't like to read. Save the book stories for the books, and save the newspaper stories for the newspapers, Warner Brothers!

4. CARRIE

Here we go with yet another book adaptation (Zzzzzz). This one comes from a piece of trash written by a first-time author and no-name horror schlock-jockey who calls himself Stephen King (King of what? Dumb, scary prom stories??). It is unfortunate that this film exists, period, but probably the biggest shame of all is that it will certainly be a career killer for its young director, Brian De Palma. As for Mr. King, I hope he enjoyed getting his gross little book published, because there is almost no way it will ever happen again. Memo to the fat cats in Hollywood: Menstrual blood = Box Office Poison.

3. NETWORK

The biggest problem with *Network* is that its premise is just too far-fetched. Director Sidney Lumet expects his viewers to believe that the human beings governing a television corporation—a *news* television corporation, at that—would value ratings and profits more than a well-informed populace. Memo to the fat cats in Hollywood: The human spirit and intellectual curiosity will always triumph over laziness and propaganda. America knows this, and so does America's news corporations!

2. TAXI DRIVER

The fat cats in Hollywood just love to throw good money after bad, I guess. Case in point: Robert De-Niro (or should I say Robert "De*Weirdo*" because he's so weird in this movie?), fresh from 1974's disastrous *The*

Godfather Part II. This guy is just too much, Columbia Pictures. America likes its film protagonists to be well-rounded and well-adjusted, not weird. Am I really expected to shell out $2.13 for a movie ticket to watch some weirdo (Robert DeNiro/Robert "De*Weirdo*") give himself a weird haircut? No thank you, fat cats (in Hollywood)! And by the way, fat cats in Hollywood, here's a memo for you: America doesn't like characters that are child prostitutes, even if they are only in supporting roles. It's unsettling.

1. ROCKY

Memo to the fat cats in Hollywood: The protagonist is supposed to win in the end!

Now, I didn't hate *every* film that was released this year. After all, there's bound to be at least one gem amongst all the pieces of crap that were crapped into the litter boxes of America's movie houses by the fat cats in Hollywood. Which brings us to…

Michael Anderson's *Logan's Run*, starring Michael York and Jenny Agutter.

Anderson's sci-fi epic was hands-down my favorite film of 1976, and though it's too early to tell right now, it might just end up being my favorite film ever. The story is not needlessly complicated (are you listening, *All the President's Men*???), the costumes are very futuristic-looking, and the special effects are as good as special effects will likely ever be. I will be shocked if *Logan's Run* does not enter the history books as the biggest and best operatic science fiction movie of the 1970s, if not all time.

Kudos to Mr. Anderson, kudos to Logan, and kudos to you, reader, if had the good sense to catch this one before it left movie theaters, the only places movies will ever be available for us to watch.

Brian Bieber is a futurist and one of America's longest running newspaper columnists, second only to his colleague (and occasional lover), Erma Bombeck.

HOW I WOULD FIGHT CERTAIN ANIMALS

L et me be clear about one thing right up top: I love animals, and I would never do anything to hurt an animal.

That said, this is how I would fight certain animals:

TARANTULA

The top thing a tarantula has going for it is its sneakiness. I can easily imagine myself talking about cool stuff with one of my good buddies, not even knowing anything is wrong until my buddy's face gets all pale and his eyes start to bug out, and I turn my head to find *a tarantula on my shoulder.*

By then, it's pretty much too late to do anything, because the tarantula is already stabbing me in the neck with its pincers, and I'm halfway dead of spider poison before I even hit the ground.

The best defense against a tarantula? Vigilance.

It seems simple, but the first thing I'd do to defeat a tarantula is *not wear so many layers of clothes that I couldn't feel a large spider crawling up to my neck.*

But let's be honest with ourselves: If the spider is already crawling up my body, then the fight is pretty much already lost—no matter how many layers of clothes I'm not wearing—because that tarantula could jab me with those pincers at any moment, on any part of my body. Before you know it, it's P.P.P.N.T. (Poison Pincer Permanent Nap Time) for me!

So how do I avoid letting the tarantula get on my body in the first place? Again, it seems simple, but check this out: *Keep an eye out for tarantulas on the ground and on the walls* (if they can crawl on walls).

I know. Duh, right?

But can tarantulas jump at me? I don't know for sure if they can jump, and if they can, how far, but for the sake of argument let's say a tarantula is jumping at me. What do I do in that scenario? Ideally, I'd have a tennis racket with me, so I could hit it with a tennis racket. A tennis racket might seem like a silly choice for a self-defense weapon, but the combination of its wide surface area and lack of wind-resistance (thanks to the netting) makes it the perfect thing with which to hit a leaping tarantula. One problem with this plan is that I don't play tennis.

KANGAROO

People talk a lot about kangaroos "boxing," but that's just an urban legend. What kangaroos do is more like kickboxing, because they use their feet to hit you. However, they also use their tails to support their weight while they do that, so their kicking is really nothing like how kickboxers kick... Maybe just forget any analogies between human martial arts and kangaroo fighting, because you'll just get confused.

Obviously, the main thing I'd have to watch out for in a fight with a kangaroo is those feet, because the kangaroo's lower body is incredibly powerful. Also, I don't know if they have any kind of claws in their feet, but if they do that's some added danger as well.

Since kangaroos are known for their jumping skills, this might seem counterintuitive, but if I had to fight a kangaroo I would try to sneak up on it (taking a page from the book of my old rival, the tarantula!) and *jump onto the kangaroo's back*. The kangaroo has a pretty long neck, so it would probably be relatively easy get my arms around it and try to choke it out.

I know what you're thinking, and of course I understand that the kangaroo would probably be jumping around all over the place trying to get me to let go. I've already thought about that, and I think that I have enough upper body strength and mental stamina to hold on to the kangaroo's neck long enough for it to pass out. It's not like it could grab me and pull me off. I mean, have you seen how short a kangaroo's arms are?

Wouldn't it be easier to try to lasso the kangaroo from a distance? Of course it would be. I could probably lasso anything from a distance if I had enough rope!

DINOSAUR

There is no way to effectively fight a dinosaur. We don't know enough about them, and there are just too many variables in that equation. We don't even know what color dinosaurs were. Did you know that some scientists now think that dinosaurs may have even had feathers? What am I supposed to do with that information?

In closing, let me just reiterate that I love animals, and would never hurt one.

VIOLENT ACTS IN APPROPRIATE SETTINGS

JIM ON THE PLAYGROUND

In grade school, there was a kid named Jim who could pop his shoulder in and out of its socket at will. I was often invited to "c'mon, feel it, man—it's so weird!" when he performed his trick. The sight and sound of it already nauseated me, so I politely declined all invitations to experience it through touch.

I think of Jim for the first time in years after my Aiki-Jujutsu instructor shows me the most efficient way to rend someone's arm from his or her shoulder socket. He actually uses the word "efficient." I've been a student of this art for only a year, and it gets more and more martial with every class I attend.

Usually I am not bothered by the casual acts of simulated violence we perform twice a week, but the thought of the strange and horrible bulge that Jim would so often summon from beneath his t-shirt has suddenly made me queasy and uncertain.

I GAVE MY COUSIN A BLOODY NOSE

At a family get-together when I was six, my cousin (then five) proudly brandished a new cap gun. It was a silver plastic cowboy six-shooter. Even as a child I was never a gun fetishist, but this one impressed me greatly.

When my cousin was occupied with other toys I picked up the pistol. I couldn't get the caps to fit correctly, so I asked him for help. He was very hot-tempered then, and flew into a rage when he saw me holding his favorite new toy. Before I knew what was happening he had me pinned to the ground and had wrenched the gun from my hands. Holding it by its barrel, he pitched his arm back to strike me with the butt end. I panicked and swung my fist wildly, somehow connecting with his nose and splaying him backward on the floor.

I began to cry when I saw the blood dribbling from his nostrils, afraid he would bleed to death. He began to cry after I did, shocked to be—for the first time—on the receiving end of a punch to the face.

I WAS BULLIED

Between grades one and seven I was bullied by a skinny boy. He was popular (or at least I took him to be), and though he was unpleasant to most, he took special care to be brutal with me. His name was Ricky, and he was ugly, with black eyes and dirty blonde hair. When he said something cruel, he spit.

HOW-TO

Kote Mawashi is performed in four steps. It involves twisting your opponent's wrist and hand inward toward his or her body while slipping under the arm and behind him or her. With each step you take, your opponent's arm is manipulated in such a way that a specific part of it is damaged:

Step one breaks the wrist.

Step two severs the connective tissue in the elbow.

Step three breaks the elbow.

Step four simultaneously dislocates the shoulder and severs much of its connective tissues.

Our instructor is a short man. He is a little portly, with small round glasses and a salt-and-pepper goatee. He tells the class what to expect aurally. He says that the arm goes "(1) *crack*, (2) *snap*, (3) *pop*, (4) *pop, snap*." His cadence is percussive. He makes learning fun.

TAXIDERMY

The room in which I punched my cousin seems dream-like when I try to remember it. The ceiling was impossibly high. The walls were covered in mounted antlers and taxidermied animal heads. A stuffed black bear stood in the corner, teeth bared, arms raised. There was a wooden spiral staircase that led up to a landing that overlooked the room, and this is where my mother and father, and aunt and uncle sat. This room was a coliseum, and my cousin and I were gladiators. This room was a cave, and we were primitives.

Logically, I know that this room doesn't exist the way I remember it. I am sure, though, that I punched my cousin, and that his nose bled and bled.

THE DOCTOR'S OFFICE

Looking puzzled by the x-rays of my shoulder, the doctor asks me to explain exactly what happened. I can't give too many details, as I wasn't aware of the injury as it was happening, but I assume it happened during a particularly rough class the week before. I speculate as to which technique would have produced the tissue damage he is describing. I tell him about *Kote Mawashi*, and he harrumphs, unimpressed.

"I would have guessed you'd been hit by a car," he says.

He doesn't mean it as a compliment, but secretly, this information pleases me very much. He thinks I'm the kind of guy who can get hit by a car and then wait a week to go in for x-rays.

IN STUDY HALL

When I was twelve Ricky challenged me to a fight after school, and I accepted. It was right before study hall, and he stopped by my desk to spit insults at me before taking his seat.

Whatcha doin', pussy? Whatcha doin'? After school, faggot. Let's go.

I was angry, and suddenly aware of how skinny he was, so I said:

Okay. Let's go. After school.

He was silent for a moment, and then a sickly, terrible grin spread across his face.

You're dead, he told me.

THE CAP GUN

My cousin is the only person I have ever really punched.

Afterward, my father explained the concept of self-defense. A little later, my cousin's parents made him apologize. It made no sense. He had a bloody Kleenex stuffed in his nose, and my hand didn't even hurt.

I don't know who owned the house or why our two families were there together. I remember there being many toys that belonged to neither my cousin nor me, but I don't remember there being any other children present. I later learned from my mother that there was no landing, no wooden staircase. The adults were two rooms away, and saw nothing.

I WAS THE ONLY ONE WHO BROUGHT A GIFT

Ricky invited me to his ninth birthday party. I didn't understand the invitation, and assumed that I must have been included by mistake, or as a joke. Even so, because of who he was, and because of who I was, it never occurred to me not to go.

His house was a few miles out of town, in a semi-residential neighborhood in which dusty fields and unpaved roads surrounded each home. On the way there I expressed my concerns about the party to my father. He wasn't dismissive, but urged me to keep an open mind. Maybe Ricky wanted to be friends. Maybe this was his way of saying he was sorry for how he had treated me in the past.

How long do I have to stay? I asked him.

I expected the party to be attended by the most popular of our classmates, because those were the circles Ricky ran in on the playground. Instead, the only children at the party were Ricky, his cousin, his two younger siblings, and me. I asked where everyone was, and he gracefully avoided the question. I gave him his present, which my father and I had purchased that morning at the drug store. It was a cheap red plastic water-powered rocket thing. I had no idea what kind of stuff Ricky liked, and didn't want to get him anything too nice, since he had been terrorizing me for as long as I had known him. He was happy with the rocket, though, and suggested we try it out.

The backyard was full of adults, who I guessed were aunts and uncles. There was food laid out on picnic tables, and a keg of beer, which I thought seemed out of place at a birthday party for a kid.

I followed Ricky and his cousin through the crowded yard to the field behind the house. As we passed, a drunk, middle-aged uncle said, "Great party, Rick!" and then laughed in a way that made me want to get away from him.

We followed the instructions, and sent the rocket high into the air, powered by a stream of pressurized water. We were going to do it again, but it landed on a rock and broke into a dozen useless pieces.

JIM REVISITED

I spend the rest of the Aiki-Jujutsu class trying to imagine the feel of a person's bones moving in the wrong direction beneath my hands. I imagine pulling a person apart at the joints. I imagine hearing the crunch of collapsing cartilage, feeling a skeleton yield under its skin, and I become light-headed.

After only one thousand repetitions, any movement—no matter how complicated or hurtful—becomes entirely reflexive, as involuntary as a sneeze.

By the end of class I am convinced that soon I will be completely numbed, able and willing to rip and twist and snap someone apart. I suddenly wish that I was ten years old again, and that Jim would ask me to touch his trick shoulder. "Yes, Jim, *yes*! It is *so* weird! Let me touch it again!"

I HAVE NIGHTMARES

When I was young, I often dreamed about being chased. I had the dreams regularly until I was about fourteen. Then I began having fight dreams. I would try to punch and kick, but my limbs were heavy and useless. A few years ago, the dreams changed again. Now I am quick, but my opponent is made of rubber, and no matter how I try, I cannot break him apart.

AFTER STUDY HALL

I was petrified. I spent most of the study hall sweating and tapping my fingers on my desk. I watched Ricky at his desk three rows ahead of me. At first I mistook his fidgeting as a sign that he was anxious to kick some ass. But as his knee jackhammered the floor and he kept looking everywhere in the room except at me, I realized that he was nervous.

After study hall, I stopped Ricky on the way to the lunchroom. I spoke to him like a lover:

This is stupid . . .

It's gone on way too long . . .

I'm so tired . . .

Let's just call it quits . . .

He didn't say anything, but nodded and offered to shake my hand. Unfortunately, we never fought after school, and nothing really changed between us.

ONE THING I DIDN'T MENTION

When I punched my cousin in the nose, it felt good.

AFTER THE ROCKET

Ricky and his cousin showed me around the neighborhood. There was a girl with big tits who lived next door, and Ricky's older brother got laid by her once. (It is worth mentioning, I think, that Ricky's older brother was rumored to be in jail for crimes unknown. Later, I would speculate that the reason Ricky was tolerated by our popular classmates was fear of the older brother, who was perpetually on the verge of parole.)

There was a family of Filipinos down the road, and Ricky's family didn't like them. I wasn't quite sure what a Filipino was, but I kept my mouth shut. There was talk of throwing rocks at the family's dog, but luckily Ricky's cousin was hungry, and suggested we go back to the house to eat. I seconded the motion. Ricky reluctantly agreed, casting dirty looks down the road toward the chain link fence that housed the Pekingese.

NICE LID

After class, the most fashionable of my Aiki-Jujutsu classmates dons a black fedora with a small red feather in the brim. As we file out of the building our instructor says to him, "Nice lid."

This groovy jazz lingo is typical. Our teacher calls clothes "threads," and digs *film noir*. When he isn't teaching efficient methods of inflicting bodily harm he teaches theater classes at a private college.

He speaks in euphemisms, but they are severe. He doesn't talk about killing. He talks about "plucking life." When he thinks that we are practicing a particularly dangerous technique without thought of its real-life ramifications, he stops the class and says:

Perform each movement with the understanding that you will be held accountable for it. We don't do things just because we can. We do them because we are absolutely sure that we must.

I LEFT THE PARTY EARLY

It turned out that one thing Ricky and I had in common was a love of cocktail wieners. We both piled our paper plates high with them and headed back into the house so that he could show me his room.

On the way, Ricky's foot caught on the living room carpet and he fell face-first to the floor, his tiny hot dogs and their sauce splattering across his t-shirt and the cream-colored shag. His mother, whose presence I hadn't noticed, stood at the other end of the living room.

Maneuvering her words around a cigarette, she said, "What the hell is wrong with you? Get off your ass and clean that shit up." Then she turned to me, squinted, and said, "Who're you?"

Not long after, I feigned illness so that I could go home. I had to ask him several times, but eventually Ricky gave me the phone and I called my father to pick me up.

It was a long wait since we were so far from my house, and for the first part Ricky sat with me on the porch. Eventually he got tired and angry, and he went back inside. When my father pulled off the gravel road and onto the driveway, I ran to meet him.

THE DOCTOR'S OFFICE REVISITED

It is evident to the doctor that I have not been faithful to my physical therapy regimen. The initial damage done to my shoulder wasn't that severe, he says. Six weeks of rest and exercises with giant rubber bands should have fixed it. He removes his glasses and frowns, and for an instant, he reminds me of Jim. The doctor asks me to describe again what I do that is so hard on my body.

I begin to explain the art I study (its beauty! its history! its science!), but become distracted by the doctor's grimace. As he clenches his jaw I note the gentle, vulnerable depression of his temple. I follow his crow's feet into the pit of his eye socket, and then out again to the peak of his nose. His brow is furrowed so that the skin is gathered directly between his eyes, where a quick strike would cause momentary blindness. I mentally trace a line down the bridge of his nose: a sharp, upward blow would produce a break and extraordinary amounts of blood. I proceed down his chin and up his jaw line, where the earlobes end and the jaw is attached so delicately to the skull. All the flaws of human construction are diagrammed neatly in the look of disapproval he wears.

He is not interested in how gracefully the tissue in my arm was torn. He only sees a mess.

"Do what you want, but the next time you hurt your shoulder, it will be much worse," he tells me.

This is the extent of his lecture, but by the time he's finished I've pummeled him a dozen times over in my mind, where I can afford to be merciless.

YOU GOTTA HAVE
A HOOK

W hat you need is a hook. If you're gonna sell re-cords, you gotta have a hook."

The sharply dressed record producer walked in small circles between his client and the studio engineer, wondering where the hell the intern was with his coffee.

His client was Smokin' Joe Thoen, a session percussionist who had played on three Grammy-winning albums, and toured for years as Sammy "The Mambo Mamba" Simek's conga man. After twenty-odd years in the business, Smokin' Joe was recording his first solo album, optimistically titled, *All You Need is Some Beats*.

"You're making great music here," the producer continued. "All you're missing is a hook."

Smokin' Joe blushed and lowered his eyes. He *did* have a hook—where is right hand used to be, before the accident. He looked to the engineer, who just sat at his mixing board, shrugged, and rolled his eyes. It was an awkward moment, one made even more awkward by the fact that the producer was blind.

"Are you listening to me?" the producer snapped. He

towered above his client, hands on hips. Cowed by the man's expensive clothing, Joe nodded vigorously.

"*Well?*" demanded the producer.

"I am, I am," Joe said a little too loudly. "So, maybe… more bells?"

"Let's listen to that last take again," the producer sighed.

He felt his way over to the mixing console, accidentally gouging the engineer's left eye in the process. The engineer clenched his jaw in pain, but made no complaint about the injury. Interpreting the man's silence as cowardice, the producer shook his head in disgust as he issued a curt apology. He had no respect for cowards.

The engineer was no coward. But he was mute, having unintentionally bitten off his own tongue at age eight. Twenty-odd years later, it was still a sore spot for him. His eyes burned with silent fury as he began the playback. The left one watered profusely.

Joe and the producer stood behind the engineer as they listened to the tracks Joe had laid down that morning. Like all of Smokin' Joe's songs, this one was an instrumental. There wasn't really a melody to speak of, but the beat—as always—was rock solid.

Usually self-conscious, Joe only felt comfortable while immersed in his work, as he was as the tape began to roll. He nodded his head and tapped out the rhythm on the metal frame of the engineer's chair—a steady *tink, tink-tink… tink, tink-tink….*

The producer made a face. "Sounds a little tinny," he said. "And can you pan the maracas left?"

The engineer and Joe exchanged a confused look. The maracas were already panned left.

Somehow the producer had gotten turned around, and was facing the wall behind them. Very gently, Joe tried to turn him by the arm, accidentally snagging his hook on the producer's sleeve in the process.

"Hey! Put that fork down!" the well-dressed, but irritable man barked. "You should be concentrating on the timbales, not lunch!"

The engineer scoffed as best he could: a little wet, and one hundred percent lips. The producer jerked his head in the general direction of the engineer. "Do you have something to say to me?"

The engineer, of course, had many things to say, to everybody—things he had been keeping to himself for twenty-odd years. He could have used sign language to say them, but he was self-conscious of his cuticles, which, he tended to pick bloody when he was nervous. Several times the engineer had tried writing a novel about a sound engineer with no tongue, but his dyslexia made it more trouble than it was worth.

So he kept quiet, and if an analog meter could measure his anger for the world, that meter's needle would be twitching itself all the way to the right, into the red. Lip quivering, the engineer acquiesced, and panned the maracas right just as the intern appeared with the producer's coffee.

"*Thank* you," the producer said pointedly. The intern quietly retreated to the other end of the room, excited to glean even some small nugget of wisdom from the three successful men before him. The producer turned his attention back to the recording. He folded his arms across his chest, resting the edge of his coffee cup against his lip, frowning and occasionally verbalizing noncommittally.

Joe found his attention drawn away from his music and to this man hired by the record company to supervise its creation. He tried to interpret the producer's grunts. He tried to follow the twitching of the man's eyebrows, the sporadic deepening of the creases at the corners of his mouth. He was searching desperately for a pattern in the producer's face, because after so many weeks in the studio, after so many miles of tape, track after track, Joe—for the first time—was unable to find a rhythm of his own.

The reels ran out to the sound of delicate, tinkling chimes, and for a short time there was silence in the studio. Moist rings darkened the underarms of Joe's t-shirt. A fat bead of sweat broke in his armpit and spilled in a tributary down his bicep and forearm, collecting momentarily in a globe at the tip of his hook before landing with a tiny splash on the toe of his right shoe.

"Hmm…" said the producer, and Smokin' Joe nearly vomited. The engineer ground his teeth and clutched a pen in his bloodless right hand. In his session notebook, beneath the heading "Production Notes," he had scrawled over and over, *"Fcuk Uyo."*

The producer turned and faced the corner, where he thought his client was standing. A thin smile spread across his face as he announced, "Fellas, I think we've got ourselves a single!"

The bile in Joe's throat receded and he exhaled audibly. The engineer closed his eyes and gently laid the pen across his notepad. For now, his wordless rage subsided. The intern sat near the door, waiting to be useful.

"Don't get me wrong," the producer said. "It still needs some work. I want you to re-record the cymbals— and really make them shimmer this time. And the bridge could use some spice… a few hand-claps, maybe."

"Or woodblocks?" suggested Joe, biting his lip.

"Hey, you're the artist," said the producer, gesturing with his coffee to an empty corner. The two shared a laugh. The engineer made a jerk-off motion.

The producer sipped his coffee and made a face. "Jesus Christ. Did I or did I not say I wanted cream?" he said to the couch… which, in all fairness, was actually pretty close to where the intern was sitting.

The intern started in his seat. "I'm sorry," he said. "I'll go get some right away."

The producer was not a patient man, and when he didn't hear the studio door open and close immediately, he grew angry. "Hop to it, junior!" he shouted at the underpaid young man. "Shake a goddamn leg, will you?"

The intern stammered an apology as he negotiated himself into the doorway and wheeled himself out into the hall.

I AM NOT HERE
TO HOLD YOUR HAND;
I AM HERE
TO RUN A BUSINESS

TO: ALL STAFF
FR: BRIAN BIEBER

I am not your mother.

If you're looking for someone to pick up your room or do your laundry, look elsewhere. And I'm not going to wipe your nose if you have the sniffles.

I'm not going to read you any bedtime stories or sing you any lullabies, and if you think that every year on your birthday I'm going to tell you where I was when I went into labor with you, then think again, because I won't, because I didn't.

I have no skin in this game, people; I'm not your mother.

I'm not going to tell you that I don't care what you do with your life as long as you're happy, but secretly wish you had pursued a field that was a little more lucrative. After all, a certain degree of happiness comes from financial security, doesn't it? Don't answer that, because I'm not really asking. Save that conversation for the Thanksgiving dinner I will not be preparing for you and your siblings. Do you even have any siblings? I wouldn't know, and if you do, none of them came out of me.

To be honest, it bothers me that I even have to say this. Aren't we all adults here?

Listen. I don't care if you're gay, and if you tell me, I won't take it really hard at first but eventually come around after I realize that you are, after all, still my child, who I conceived, carried, birthed and suckled, and that the gender of those to whom you are sexually attracted has no real bearing on any of that. And even though it would mean that any of the grandchildren I had always hoped for would likely not be related to me biologically, I would get over it. None of that applies to this situation. I'm not your mother, and if I was, I would be too young to be a grandmother anyway.

Are you having your first period? Not my department. Come to me if you have payroll questions, but save the tampon talk for a more appropriate conversation partner. Like your mother.

Are you Catholic? I don't care that you didn't get confirmed. Are you Jewish? I don't give a shit whether your spouse is, too.

I didn't marry your father out of some outdated sense of moral obligation. I don't get tense when the subject of your birth date or my wedding anniversary come up, afraid that whoever is asking will perform that simple, embarrassing calendar arithmetic. I don't even know when your birthday is; that generic greeting card you get every year comes straight from HR. I don't read it before I sign it. Last year I didn't even sign it. Does that sound like something a mother would forget to do?

So, please: If you use a community dish, take a minute to wash it, and put it back in the break room cupboard.

Thank you.

PLEASE HELP ME
FIND MY BACKPACK

Please help me find my backpack.

"Whoa, whoa, *whoa!* Slow down, Brian. Take a deep breath. Stop crying, and put your shirt back on. It's just a backpack. It can't be that important, can it?"

You know what? By even just saying that right now, you embarrassed yourself, and you don't even know it.

Why? What's in it? Oh, I don't know, let me see... Just my entire life!!!

Let me explain something to you. I don't work in an "office" or a "home office" or a "mobile office" or in a building that is in an "office park." I am a man of action, and I live my life on the go. If I had to, I could live for three days in the wild with nothing but the items inside my backpack. I kinda really need to find it.

So I'm coming to you, hat in hand (because I currently do not have a backpack in which to keep my hat), asking for your help in finding my backpack.

"Well, what does your backpack look like, Brian? How can we help you find it if we don't know what it looks like?"

How dare you.

My backpack is nylon. Pattern? Camo. Duh.

Color? Purple and green. Yeah. Joker-style.

And, yep, it's a JanSport. But I ripped the label off, because I'm not one to brag.

I know that there are a lot of purple and green camo nylon JanSport backpacks out there. (Why do think I bought it? There's more than one kind of camo, friend!) So if you think you've found my backpack, I am giving you permission to open it for the sole purpose of positively identifying it as mine. I know *exactly* what is inside, and I will know if *anything* is missing.

The following is a complete list of every item inside of my missing backpack:

Six 22 oz. protein shakes—4 mixed, one still powdered, one *possibly* still powdered

One notebook of ideas for rap lyrics in case I ever want to become a rapper. (This is really important because it is extremely difficult to replace ideas, and I haven't memorized almost any of those rap lyrics. The only ones I can kind of remember are "something, something mountain tops/something, something karate chops" and "talking chalky like a chalk-thing/rolling up on birds of prey like my man Stephen Haw-king")

Eleven dollars in petty cash (2 fivers and a single)

Five dollars in emergency cash (1 fiver sewn into the lining of the left strap)

One cool archery magazine I found that has a picture of a guy on the front with one of those really complicated bows and arrows, and he's pointing the arrow right at the camera.

Please note: that magazine is super badass, and it's really important that I get it back, because I want find someone with a camera to recreate that picture with me in it instead of the badass magazine guy so I can put the picture on my website.

If you find my backpack, or any of its contents, PLEASE text a photo of it to 605 323-9247. Once those protein shakes are mixed they get really gross if you don't drink them within like 72 hours.

Also, if you don't know where my backpack is, but you know how to use Photoshop, it would be really cool of you to put my face on the body of a badass guy with a bow and arrow so I could at least put that on my website.

Thank you! I really appreciate all of your help!

For Photoshop use only.

DOCTORS

Oh my god. Oh my god, thank you. What did you do? How did you save my baby?"

The baby's mother and father are sitting in comfortable chairs, on the other side of my desk, in my office. The father doesn't say anything. He just sits there with his hands on his face, his elbows on his knees, shaking. The mother is sobbing hysterically.

I, on the other hand, am relaxed. I lean back in my chair and light a cigarette. I am a doctor; I have hysterical people in my office all the time.

"How did I save your baby?" I pause, take a pull on my Marlboro, and consider my words. "To start with, I sewed his arm back on."

Of course, it's more complicated than that, but she's a social studies teacher, for Christ's sake. He's a computer programmer. What am I supposed to tell them? The brand of thread I used?

There are more thank yous and more tears, and the mother hugs me tightly over my arms. I always try to be sensitive, but I don't like being touched, so I extricate myself from her quickly. Once they've both pulled themselves together I give them directions to the ICU, and move them out the door.

A little before noon I pop my head into Chad's office, two floors down, and ask if he has plans for lunch. He folds up the morning paper, grabs his jacket, and we're on our way. I light another Marlboro in the elevator, and Chad asks if he can bum one. I have more than half a pack left so it's not really a big deal, but lately Chad has been making a habit of mooching. Sometimes I want to shake him: *You're a cardiologist, Chad! Can't you afford to buy your own smokes once in a while?*

We eat at a little bistro not far from the physicians' office building. Right away Chad starts flirting with our waitress, but she's not receptive. It's a desperate kind of flirting. He laughs loud for no reason, and his eyes bulge like a lunatic's. Chad got married last fall. He's terrified that it's made him invisible and irrelevant. I'm a trauma surgeon, not a psychiatrist, but I'm willing to bet that at the end of lunch he'll tip the waitress thirty percent, and it will make him feel both ashamed and aroused.

As we eat, Chad tells me about his trip to the consumer electronics trade show in Las Vegas. Next winter, he tells me, there's going to be a one hundred-inch hi-definition LED TV on the market. There was a demo model on the trade show floor playing scenes from *Top Gun*, and Chad says it kicked ass. He glances around, leans forward, lowers his voice, and says, "There was a second demo TV..."

Then he raises an eyebrow and mouths, *"upstairs."*

The upstairs he's referring to is the second floor of the convention center. The first floor is crowded with kiosks displaying the latest innovations in home entertainment: TVs, cameras, home theater systems. The second floor— the floor that gets three times as much foot traffic—is home to the world's largest annual porn convention. The second floor is packed wall-to-wall with pornographers pushing their wares. Directors rub elbows with producers and distributors. Stars and starlets promote new releases by signing glossy, 8x10 black-and-white head-, chest-, ass-, and crotch-shots. There are TV monitors mounted everywhere, with the hundred-inch LED as a kind of centerpiece. "You would not believe the video they were showing on that screen," Chad says wickedly. "A*maz*ing."

I nod as he talks, but Chad has told me about the trade show many times before, and I'm preoccupied with the baby I sewed together this morning. It's the kind of thing I do every day, but sometimes—pretty often lately—I can't stop thinking about how implausible it is that a person like me can do such inhumanly powerful things. All of these messes of skin, muscle, fat, blood, and bone that we clean up on a daily basis.... I'm not one of those doctors who think he's a god or anything, but I wonder sometimes: if there is a God, is He even relevant anymore, with people like Chad and me around?

"I don't even know how she got it all in there!" Chad giggles. The way he goes on about these movies, you'd think he was a gynecologist.

Our waitress comes to clear our plates, and Chad

stops talking abruptly. In the deepest parts of my brain I am stitching his mouth shut, no anesthesia.

"How's Stephanie?" I ask him.

He looks at me hatefully.

I have only one afternoon appointment: a follow-up with a seventeen-year-old boy who was in a car wreck a couple of weeks ago. He was drunk or fell asleep at the wheel or something, and ended up flipped over in a ditch on the edge of some farmer's lot.

I was able to staple most of his face back onto his head, but he had been driving with the window down, so his arm was a lost cause. It was missing for five days after the accident, until the farmer's dog showed up with it at the back door. By then it was four-and-a-half days too late.

I shake the kid's remaining hand, and exchange pleasantries with his parents. We're all sunshine and smiles—except for the kid, who won't be able to smile for another week without the risk of his face falling back off. In a way—and of course only in a very abstract way—I envy him.

The kid is horrifying to look at, but only compared to a person with a normal face. Compared to how he looked before I got hold of him, I'm almost telling the truth when I say to him, "Lookin' good...."

I have him sit down while I light a cigarette, and then I begin my examination. I squat in front of him and lay my thumbs on his cheekbones, my fingers splayed out with the tips resting on the metal sutures running from his temples down his jaw line. Very gently, I prod and massage his face. The flesh is rubbery and pale, and still very loose; it gives slightly, and slides just the tiniest bit across his skull. I could tease his face into any number of hilarious expressions that would be impossible to produce on a healthy human's… but I took an oath when I received my license, and that oath says that such displays of broad physical comedy are unethical. Sometimes I think the loneliest thing a person can be is a doctor.

I know pretty much immediately that the surgery didn't take. The kid's face will turn yellow, then purple, then a moldy black. It will fall off sooner rather than later.

Sometimes, that's how it goes.

The best I can do now is get the kid a rubber mask like the one Tom Cruise wore in *Vanilla Sky*. I'm not a social worker.

I finish the exam with a wink and a playful little slap to the kid's cheek, because, honestly, at this point it's not like I'll hurt anything. I sit back behind my desk, take a long drag, and exhale.

I could think of this as a tragedy—this kid who will soon lose his face, whose arm was found in a ditch by some hillbilly's dog. I could stay up late tonight thinking: Could I have placed the staples closer together, or farther apart? Should I have used more gauze? If you let them, these things will eat you up. So I don't let them.

The kid and his parents are looking at me. The looks of expectation they wear—the nervous hope—sets my teeth on edge. The really unfair thing is that they don't know about the baby I sewed together this morning, and because of HIPAA laws, I can't tell them.

"Well?" the kid's father asks me. He is literally wringing his hands in his lap.

The way the kid is looking at me from behind his swollen and discolored face, I'd guess he already knows.

A rubber Tom Cruise mask won't look so bad on him.

"Well…" I pause to snub out my cigarette, and I choose my words carefully before I address the parents. "He'll be fine."

I smile at the kid. "You'll look fine."

SCIENCE FICTION

If you're from the future, how come I can see you?" she asked.

"I never said I was an *invisible* time traveler," he replied.

She narrowed her eyes, and smirked. *Well played, time traveler.*

TALES OF EROTICA: CHUCK NORRIS & ME

Everybody loves getting turned on, and everybody loves high-kicking martial arts action.

So I'm going to tell you about the very first heavy-petting session I engaged in with my first girlfriend when I was sixteen. But for the sake of confidentiality, instead of using her real name, I'm going to refer to her as action star Chuck Norris. Likewise, any personal details about my ex-girlfriend that might implicate her directly will be changed to indicate achievements earned by Mr. Norris.

For example, instead of referring to Madeline as a junior varsity basketball cheerleader I will refer to her as an international karate champion. And when I say "star of TV's *Walker: Texas Ranger*" I'll really mean "supporting cast member in a 1996 high school production of *Jesus Christ: Superstar.*"

Any references to sexual activities we engaged in will be disguised as martial arts maneuvers. I won't say Maddie was the first girl I ever French kissed. I'll say, "Chuck Norris kicked me so hard in the mouth that I had to have my jaw wired shut."

When mentioning details that still embarrass me, I will go on and on with analogies that—if you really think about them—make sense, but are pretty difficult to follow. I won't sheepishly admit that even at age 15 she was more experienced than I was. I'll ask you to imagine a younger Chuck Norris, not yet a master of his art—maybe a brown belt—leading one of the newer karate students in basic "block, step, kick" exercises during the warm-up time before class, while the teacher is stretching. I won't tell you that before that afternoon on my parents' couch I had kissed only one other girl—awkwardly—on the cheek, and was quickly, but gently rebuffed. Instead, I'll casually share an anecdote about the time I sparred with Steven Seagal, who let me take a couple swings at him, but quickly got bored, and didn't even waste the energy it would take to break a few of my bones.

The thing about Chuck Norris is that he is not the least bit pretentious. He is not without moments of gracelessness—sometimes overextending a kick, or putting too much of his upper body behind a punch. His form is not nearly as fun to watch as Jet Li's exhausting acrobatics, and it is not quite as pretty as the phony grace of Jean-Claude Van Damme, whose elegance belies technique that is beautiful to look at, but entirely useless in a real combat situation. More than anything, Chuck Norris is effective, and he is not self-conscious. I, on the other hand, was deathly afraid of getting a hickey.

I ran into Chuck three years after we stopped fighting regularly. We were both home from our respective colleges during a holiday break. We went to a movie one night, out to coffee another. Finally, the night before I was to return to school, our mutual animosity got the best of us and a fight broke out in the guest bedroom of my parents' house, where we had been watching *Saturday Night Live*. We had both trained hard in the previous years and were eager to demonstrate the new moves we had learned. In our eagerness, of course, we disregarded technique and the bout quickly turned into a brawl, our limbs flailing wild, a mess. In this way, the battle was much like our first, but not nearly as sweet.

Afterward, I walked Chuck out to his car, feeling defeated. I leaned in close to the star of the box office flop *Firewalker*, and asked if he was sure that this was okay. He smiled at me tenderly, placed a hand on my cheek—a hand that had smashed pine boards and bricks, had shattered giant blocks of ice—and then he leapt into the air and delivered a devastating flying roundhouse kick to my skull.

MY DJ

I have to take the bus to the doctor's office, because some drunk rear-ended me last week on my way home from an after-bar. It's morning rush hour, so of course my DJ and I have to stand. He doesn't have a stable surface to set his turntables on, so his records keep skipping all over the place. I almost don't care; while certainly not wack, the shit he's spinning this morning is a far cry from dope. The unimpressed looks our fellow passengers are exchanging tell me I'm not alone in my assessment.

My DJ lays down some real hardcore shit while the doctor tells me the lump on my left testicle is just a benign cyst. The doctor starts to give me a little lecture about the importance of performing monthly checks on myself, but it's hard to keep a straight face, because my DJ is wearing a surgical mask and pretending to scratch his records with a tongue depressor.

I'm really relieved about not having testicular cancer, and I have to restrain myself from singing along with the words to the sample my DJ drops every twelve measures or so. The doctor gives me a little plastic card to hang in my shower that shows me how to check for lumps. *Motherfucker say what*, I mouth to the beat. My DJ encourages the doctor to throw his hands up, but the doctor declines.

At the auto body shop, my DJ goes crazy with the crossfades. The Corolla's entire rear bumper is going to have to be replaced, not to mention the left taillight. I know the mechanic has to be fronting with the estimate he gives, but my DJ is kicking rhythms that are superfresh, and the drunk is well insured, so I don't even really care. Before long, I'm waving my hand in the air, and I can tell the mechanic wants to bounce with me, but instead he tells my DJ to move his tables so the guy can pull my car into the garage.

We take Kelly's car to dinner, and I suggest True Thai, because it's her favorite. She orders something with pineapple and noodles that has a little pepper icon next to it on the menu. I order the *pad thai*, mild. Behind me, at the next table, my DJ spins some old, crazy bossa nova 78. I don't know where he finds this stuff. He told me he has over 5,500 records in his collection: boxes upon boxes in his basement. He hasn't even listened to most of them yet.

True Thai is a little cramped, but most of the restaurant's other patrons recognize my DJ's skills, and—to varying degrees—they dance to the rhythm in their chairs. Even Kelly, who usually likes things quiet, can't help but bob her head as she wipes her mouth and tells me she's moving out. This is totally unexpected, and more than a little wack, in my opinion. Things have been tense lately, but moving out? I almost hope there's someone else, but that's not it. Apparently, being with no one is better than staying with this emcee.

My DJ takes the news in stride, and in a misguided show of solidarity, cuts seamlessly into a slightly misogynist early 90s dance number. It seems like I can feel the whole room feeling sorry for me as Kelly and I quietly finish our meals. Then the manager tells my DJ he either has to order something or pack up his gear, because he's taking up a pretty big table. I can't even imagine how this situation could be any less dope.

HOW TO NOT LIE
AT THE BLOOD BANK

She was halfway down the list of donor questions before the lady at the blood bank asked me, "Have you ever been given money or drugs in exchange for sex?"

"Money *or* drugs?" I replied. We shared a little laugh.

"But seriously," she said. "Have you ever been given money or drugs in exchange for sex?"

"Given?" I replied. "I'll have you know I earned every gram!"

We laughed together again. She checked the box for *NO* on the form, and I leaned back in my chair, my conscience clean.

AMPHETAMINE
TWICE MONTHLY

Amphetamine," I told her, "twice a month." I really wanted her to like me.

She looked up from the clipboard in her lap, below the edge of the table, where I couldn't see it. "Twice a month?" she asked.

I nodded gravely.

I was lying. Not just about the frequency, but about taking the drug at all. I'd never used amphetamines—or any other drugs, for that matter. Except for morphine once when I was in the emergency room with a kidney stone. And alcohol lots of times, if you count that. I even avoided aspirin.

"That's not as frequent as many amphetamine users," she said.

"It's still a nasty habit," I replied, my expression remaining grave. I wasn't proud of my imaginary problem.

"Yes. I suppose so." She checked something on her clipboard, which made me nervous. "Do you use any other drugs recreationally?"

"Just some weed," I said.

"Marijuana?"

"The Chronic, yes." I nodded gravely.

Check. Check.

What was she checking?

She smiled at me: warm, but professional. She had lovely brown eyes. "How often do you smoke marijuana?"

"Every day," I said, and immediately regretted it. "But sometimes not at all, too."

She looked up from her clipboard.

She was a graduate student researching recreational drug use among university students. Even though I don't use drugs, I called the number on her flyer, because I was thinking about auditioning for an improv troupe, and it seemed like a good way to practice my skills. I had no idea she would be so attractive.

"Um," I said, "On average it comes out to, maybe, twice a week." Why did I keep using the word "twice"? "Or sometimes once."

Her forehead wrinkled. "Can you.. Hm." She pinched the skin between her eyes, took a breath. "Okay," she said, "Let's-"

"I meant 'a month'," I said.

"What?"

"I meant to say I smoke pot twice a month. Like the amphetamine. Not twice a week." I puffed out a little laugh. "That would be crazy."

I wanted her to like me, and I was starting to feel guilty. Maybe I was screwing up her thesis. She was going to be a doctor of something, and what was I? An aspiring improvisational comedian? A waiter in a natural foods restaurant? Some random university student?

No. I lied about being a student, as well.

"What kind of doctor?" I asked. She was in the middle of asking me something, so it took her a moment to respond.

"Well, a physician, eventually," she said. "I'm specializing in addiction medicine."

"*Nice,*" I said, nodding and smiling big. It was completely inappropriate.

In my head, we were far beyond the interview. We were dating, an item, getting serious. This is the part I skipped to: About to have an important discussion. Parked in front of her apartment building, in my car. The big conversations always happen in a car. Her brow is wrinkled, her lovely brown eyes are heavy with—obviously—love… but she is upset.

Because this isn't how things were supposed to go. I was supposed to be a fling, a couple of fun nights. But a couple of nights suddenly turned into a couple of weeks, and then months, and then here we are, sitting in my car. Her hands flutter in front of her. *This can't happen*, she says. She has her thesis to think of… and is it even ethical for her to be sleeping with her research subject? And though I hear everything she's saying, and though I nod my head in agreement, I am confident that I won't be going home tonight. And when I wake up in the morning her arm will be draped across my stomach and she'll still be asleep, smiling into my neck, her breath tickling… And that is how it will be every morning from now on. She will finish her thesis, and it will be lauded among her colleagues, and her advisors will raise their eyebrows, impressed. We will talk about having children someday, but for now we will simply enjoy being together, just the two of us. We will travel to countries it would never occur to me to visit before I met her. During holiday visits, her father will squeeze my shoulder and nod approvingly. We will have a house. We will have a dog, and we will have those children we talked about. There will be two of them, and they will look like us, and they will be like us in all of the good ways. We will garden together—I will learn how to garden, and it will turn out that I am a natural! We will drink a glass of red wine with dinner most nights. She will retire from her practice, and we will move someplace warm. New advancements in medical technology will keep us healthy and alive much longer than people live now, and we will spend all of those extra decades with our fingers entwined, smiling to ourselves and at one another... I know all of this because as she says, "This can't happen this can't happen," she is leaning toward me, across the center console of my car. Her hand is moving toward my cheek. Her lovely brown eyes are heavy with—obviously—love!

"Dry mouth? Insomnia?" she asked.

I had no idea what she was talking about.

"I'm sorry?"

"I asked you about side effects," she said. "Do you ever experience dry mouth, or insomnia? Any other side effects?"

I wished I hadn't told her all of those lies about my pretend drug use. She was too good to be with some dry-mouthed junkie.

She was waiting for an answer. I was chewing on my lower lip—something a junkie would probably do. I cursed myself silently and stopped.

"I could stop if I really had to," I told her.

She opened her mouth a little, leaned back a little. "Oh… Oh. This isn't- "

"I mean if, you know, if I really—in reality—had to quit, I think I could do it. I could stop, and I would do it—easily—for the right person…"

"Listen," she said, looking at her hands, looking at her clipboard. Not at me. "I'm not here to judge you. If you'd like to talk to someone, I can give you numbers to call. I can-"

I was shaking my head; my eyes were closed. She didn't get it. Didn't she get it? She didn't get it at all…

"No," I said. "I just want…" My elbows were on the table, my hands lying useless between us. I wanted us to be sitting in my car, outside of her apartment building.

"Hey," she said. Her voice was soft, like gauze. She put her hand on top of mine. "If you want help, we can get you help…"

Yes! I thought. *Yes! Help me.*

Now we were looking at each other, and her lovely brown eyes were heavy. But it was—quite obviously—the wrong kind of heavy. Not yet desperate, but getting there, I weighed her pity against what I was already calling my love. I moved my mouth, dry, said nothing.

PRETEND TO BE GOOD

She was sniffling as I fell asleep, wiping her nose in hurried, embarrassed strokes. I thought she just had a head cold, but by the time I woke up she was choking on great heaving sobs. The seats were so close together that I could feel her shuddering against my arm. The older woman on her left stared out the tiny window with purpose, cold and still as marble.

I don't fly often, and I was unsure of my role in the scene. Should I ask what's wrong? Just leave her alone? It was a new etiquette, like not checking my voice mail during takeoff: *I didn't know.*

There had been some confusion with my ticket during the boarding process, and I was the last on the plane. The flight was booked solid and I had an aisle seat, so I was cranky as I shuffled down the fuselage. I winced every time I accidentally bumped someone's elbow or knocked my carry-on against someone's head, knowing that soon I would share their fate. Soon I would have my toes clipped by the beverage cart.

My mood lifted considerably when I saw my seatmate. She looked to be in her early thirties, with dark features and a toned, athletic build. Her eyes were enormous and green. Her mouth was small, but full. She could have been in a toothpaste commercial.

We exchanged polite smiles as I settled into my seat. I gestured for her to take the armrest. She said thanks, "but we can probably just share."

This, I thought, is how letters to *Penthouse* begin. I introduced myself.

"I'm Victoria," she replied. She was even smiling a little as she said it.

I was looking forward to some small talk, and then two-and-a-half hours of flirting and casual, but mildly intimate physical contact. Instead, she opened her cell phone, and (without regard for the rule) checked her voice mail. Then she arranged a small pillow behind her neck, sniffled a little, and closed her eyes. With a sigh, I opened my book—about the last man on Earth waging war against a world overrun by vampires—and quickly dozed off.

Now, two hours later, only half-awake, and confronted with Victoria's weeping, I was nearly paralyzed. I hated myself for keeping quiet, for staring dumbly at the aisle's worn carpeting.

I was saved by the beverage cart. Her eyes damp, her nose running, Victoria ordered her first chardonnay. Before the attendant could move the cart to the next aisle, Victoria ordered her second. When the attendant picked up my empty Pepsi can, she ordered a third.

She had just enough time for one more before the pilot announced the beginning of our descent. The weather was getting bad, and things were going to feel "a little shaky" as we came down. Even as he turned off the PA system, the plane lurched violently. Victoria let out a little yelp and clutched our armrest. She flushed and said, "I really don't like flying."

I smiled and said something not memorable, not as clever as I would have liked.

She smiled back anyway, the lids on her great green eyes heavy. Her mouth settled into a curl. "Are you from Chicago?" she asked me, the smell of wine heavy and cheap on her breath.

This is the beginning of a very specific kind of fantasy for many young men: An attractive, slightly older stranger; close quarters; an unquestionably temporary romantic connection... At first it was the easiest conversation I'd ever engaged in, because it's one I'd rehearsed mentally a dozen times over in every airport on this trip. *How long is your layover?* a beautiful stranger might ask. *Why don't we grab a drink together? I don't live far from here...*

"I'm just passing through," I told Victoria. It was corny, but I liked the way it felt coming out of my mouth. It made me feel like someone who owned more than one piece of luggage.

"Well, it sounds like the weather's getting pretty nasty," she said, twisting in her seat so that our arms touched. "I hope your connecting flight isn't canceled."

She smirked a little and raised one eyebrow, as if to say, *I actually* do *hope your flight is canceled.*

"Guess I'll have some time to kill if it is," I said, maintaining eye contact in opposition to every fiber of my being. We were suddenly both reading from the same hackneyed script, and I didn't want to screw it up. I saw a movie once where two strangers had sex in a janitor's closet at the airport. Could that be me? Was I the kind of guy who could have sex at the airport? My stomach fluttered.

"Anyone waiting for you at home?" she asked me. It was ridiculous!

I told her no, I didn't have anyone waiting for me. Technically my sister would be waiting to pick me up at the airport later that evening, in Minneapolis, but that seemed like an unnecessary clarification.

"What about you?" I asked. And this is where things began to fall apart.

She paused for a beat. She sniffed once. "I have two little boys at home," she said. "With their dad."

This certainly wasn't in *my* script.

The curl of her mouth softened as she went on. "I was looking forward to being away for a few days, but I already miss them—the kids, I mean. You know what I mean?"

I nodded as if I knew what she meant. I thought about my studio apartment. How I had forgotten to take the trash out before I left. How I knew that when I got home the whole place would smell rotten.

Victoria was looking past me now, her irises even

greener for the broken blood vessels framing them. She was quiet for a moment, thinking of her little boys maybe, or maybe it was just that she was drunk. But her reverie was soon broken by another steep dip of the plane. She gasped, and squeezed my wrist, letting her hand linger long enough for us both to look at it. The cabin shuddered, then relaxed.

"It's tough," she said, finding my eyes, and finding her place again in my script, "because I'm going through this divorce…"

I know this sounds great, but I was rattled. When I said that I was sorry to hear about her divorce, I was annoyed that I kind of meant it, which had an adverse effect on my flirting.

"That sounds hard," I said lamely.

She nodded. "Yeah."

I nodded. "Yeah… Well, hang in there, I guess."

Hang in there? I didn't even *deserve* to get laid in a janitor's closet! My eyes wandered back to the book on my lap. I began to wonder how that guy could possibly kill all those vampires…

"No one tells you," she said, and I bristled. I was shocked at how quickly I had lost interest in what she had to say. I turned back to Victoria, and feigned attentiveness, pretended to be someone good.

"There's no one to tell you how it will be after," she went on. "You just do what you think everyone does, and all of a sudden you've got these kids and things are still all messed up and you're just trapped there. No one tells you that might happen…" Now it sounded like she was reading from a different kind of script—something made for TV.

"I love my boys," she went on. "They're everything to me, but I just..."

She paused, and then she actually said this to me:

"I just need my vacation to be a little longer."

Her pupils expanded and contracted. I could feel myself coming in and out of focus. Maybe we would find a closet together after all.

The plane bucked once more, and then seemed to bounce a few times before the landing gear caught on the runway. For a moment we seemed to be going too fast. The cabin was silent, its passengers still. Two hundred pairs of lungs frozen, full of stale, recycled air. Bracing ourselves for the end of everything.

And then we were at the gate.

Victoria and I exchanged relieved glances. I hadn't realized my heart was pounding. I tried not to notice the rise and fall of her chest as she regained her breath, but she was wearing one of those tight, scoop-neck sweaters.

"Close one," I said, and made a show of wiping pretend sweat from my forehead.

We waited for most of the other passengers to deboard before we stood from our seats. We had arrived too soon. Nothing had been established. We had no plan. We looked at each other again, our mouths straining at the corners. I pulled her bag from the overhead for her, and walked behind as she navigated herself through the umbilicus to the terminal, swaying just a little.

O'Hare was a mess. The weather had filled it with

people trying to check in for flights that had been long since delayed or canceled. Victoria and I pushed through the mass of people, and made our way to the bank of monitors listing departures and cancellations. She ran her finger down the screen, stopping on my flight number. We both looked at it for a while, considering the implications.

"So…"

"So," she said, turning to me, her eyes seeming suddenly clearer, more sober.

I looked back at the monitor, hoping for a cue of some kind. "Uh…"

"I suppose I should try to find myself a cab," she said. At first I couldn't tell if she was asking a question.

When I turned back to her, she was already wading into the sea of crabby travelers and their rolling luggage. I began to follow, but the crowd folded in and consumed her almost immediately. I quickened my pace for a few steps. I even opened my mouth, but her name didn't make it out. I tried to calculate the value of finding her and saying goodbye. I wondered whether it had been a pleasure meeting me.

ANOTHER CLOWN

Y ou fucked another clown?" Sparky's voice broke as
    he said it.

Pinky sat silently on the couch, her eyes fixed on
her enormous red shoes. Sparky walked in tight circles in
front of her, eyes twitching, hands fisted—a nervous animal dressed in rainbow wig and spinning bow tie. They
had just made love that morning. At the time he thought
nothing of the tension in her frame as he held her. Now,
of course, it seemed obvious. He clenched his jaw and
repeated the question, his voice hard now like a juggling
pin, cold now like seltzer.

Ever so slightly, she nodded.

He squeezed his eyes tight, suppressed a tremble.
He asked her where. He asked her when. He didn't have
to ask who.

She began to sob. She laid her face in her hands. She
put her elbows in her lap. Loudly, Sparky told her to tell
him where, and when. He wasn't a violent clown, but in
his anger he became aware of the fragile boundaries of

slapstick. He scared himself. He asked again—this time quieter.

It was in Blinky's car, two nights prior. They had too much to drink. They were dancing. Things got out of hand.

Sparky closed his eyes. He collapsed into the love seat across the room. Pinky was looking up at him, tears streaming, big red nose running, her face paint a mess.

It was a mistake! she said. *A stupid mistake! Please!* she sobbed.

Sparky grimaced. *Please?* What does that even *mean?*

For a long time he looked at the carpet. Pinky sniffed, and wiped her eyes.

Sparky had always told himself he would never stand for this; he would never be made to look like a fool. He tried to imagine tonight with Pinky. He would sleep on the couch tonight. But tomorrow? The next day? He wondered how long until he could look at her again and not see her sprawled out across the back seat of Blinky's tiny automobile. Her silk coveralls wrinkled and undone. The white foundation Sparky had helped apply to her face that morning reduced to a sweaty, post-coital smear of grease paint. Could he love her again the way he had loved her yesterday?

Not knowing, but afraid, he let her come to him. He let her cradle his curly, rainbowed head in her arms. He let himself be soothed.

OB-LA-DIDN'T

The wooden folding chair is too small for Desmond. He crosses his legs. He uncrosses his legs. He turns slightly, hoping to minimize the surface area of his ass in contact with the seat, but succeeds only in knocking his knee into Molly, who nudges him discretely, but with purpose. She purses her lips and cocks her head toward the gazebo, where their only daughter, Ms. Suzanne Jones, is a few words away from becoming Mrs. Suzanne Merchant. Desmond ignores Molly's glare. He crosses his legs again.

At the center of the gazebo, Suzanne's fingertips are perched in the Merchant boy's left palm. A thin gold band trembles in the callused, stubby fingers of his right hand. Though he stands a full head taller than Suzanne, the Merchant boy looks at her from beneath his brow. He licks his lips and clears his throat as he repeats after the reverend. Molly wipes her eyes in a single, hurried stroke. Desmond uncrosses his legs and straightens his back. Still no relief.

The gazebo sits atop a slight incline, so the bride and groom are visible to all in attendance. It is late in the afternoon and the sun is low enough to tint Suzanne's dress amber. Desmond does not hear the vows as his daughter speaks them. Around and behind him he hears women sniff and men cough. He hears two waiters whispering at the clubhouse door fifty yards behind him. He hears the distant scrape of tree branches in the wind. But when Suzanne—who is standing not ten feet from him—pledges to spend her life with that kind but stupid lump of a man standing in front of her, Desmond can only see her lips move. He looks away.

The Merchant boy kisses his new wife. The guests stand and applaud. Jonathan Jones—Suzanne's brother and the groom's best man—places two fingers in his mouth and blows a shrill wolf whistle. There are scattered chuckles among the wedding guests. Molly smiles and shakes her head. Desmond's forehead creases. He wonders where his son learned to do something so common.

This is the same garden in which he and Molly were married three decades before, but the decision to use it was not sentimental. It is the most reasonably priced outdoor location in the city.

The bride and groom walk down an aisle formed by parallel rows of marigolds. Today the flowers look less brilliant to Desmond than they did thirty summers ago. The spaces between them seem wider: rows of dirt interrupted by accidental spots of color. Suzanne beams at her parents as she passes. Molly swipes a crumbling tissue across her eyes. Desmond twists the corners of his mouth upward, hoping his expression does not look as grotesque as it feels.

Inside the clubhouse there are two dozen circular tables draped in blood-red linens arranged around a small dance floor. Musicians in tuxedos tune their guitars in a distant corner. At the front of the room the wedding party faces their guests from the head table. Desmond and Molly share a table with their son-in-law's parents, Richard and Tammy Merchant, who are part-owners of a small, inauthentic Indian restaurant. As such, they are the reason that Desmond is eating something called "Tammy's Tandoor-ific Chicken" at his daughter's wedding dinner.

Also sitting at their table is a girl called Abby, who has come as Jonathan's date. After seeing Abby abandoned by Jonathan for the head table, Molly invited the girl to sit with her and Desmond, despite having only met her earlier this afternoon. Abby's smile is constant, but her eyes are anxious. Molly casually places her hand on Abby's and insists that Abby tell her where she has her hair done. Soon enough the two women are shoulder-to-shoulder, and Abby cannot stop giggling as Molly regales her with stories of Jonathan's troubled adolescence. Desmond, meanwhile, is trapped in a discussion with the elder Merchants about the cheapest, quickest way to prepare *mung dahl*.

It had not occurred to Desmond that, as the best man, Jonathan would be delivering a toast. So when his son stands at his seat and begins knocking a spoon against his wineglass, Desmond stiffens in his chair. The last time he heard Jonathan give any kind of speech was two summers ago at his grandfather's eightieth birthday party. Jonathan had concluded that one with a joke about a man cursed with testicles growing from his forehead. Afterward, Jonathan boasted that the politely received testicle joke "is always a sure thing." Desmond glances at Mr. and Mrs. Merchant, and braces himself.

The testicle joke, however, never comes. Instead, Jonathan's remarks are brief and thoughtful. He says he is happy that his friend has become his brother, and notes that love has transformed his sister from a pretty girl into a beautiful woman. He speaks of romantic love in simple, earnest terms. He raises his glass to the couple. It is a man's gesture—one he did not learn from Desmond. The guests applaud. There is no need for polite chuckles.

The elder Merchants smile at Desmond as they clap. Richard squeezes his shoulder. Desmond nods once, quickly. If only a man could love his son as simply as he loves his daughter.

Molly has to wipe her eyes once again. Abby looks at Jonathan in a way that gives Desmond pause. Molly leans over and whispers something in Abby's ear, and Abby turns red. Upon meeting her, Desmond had dismissed her as simply a girl with a pretty face. Now he tries to look at her with a young man's eyes. He thinks that maybe a pretty face is good enough. As a start, at least.

The band enthusiastically plays all the songs they are

expected to play. Everybody is pleasantly drunk—Desmond included. Most of the tables are deserted, save the blazers and purses slung over chair backs. Desmond and Molly are among the few sitting. Desmond has had his dance with Suzanne. Molly has danced with her new son-in-law. She leans into Desmond now, her arm draped over his shoulders. Desmond stares onto the dance floor at the Merchant boy, who leads Suzanne awkwardly by the hips.

As the song ends, Desmond watches Suzanne leave her husband to speak with the bandleader, and then stride across the dance floor toward her parents. She pulls her mother by the arm, pleading. Just one song, she says. For old time's sake. Molly looks genuinely terrified. She tries to refuse, but when the guests see what is happening, the cheering begins. Molly relents and steps onto the collapsible aluminum stage, her cheeks ablaze. She consults with the band, and clears her throat before approaching the microphone.

She is hesitant for the first few bars of the ballad, and her voice trembles on the end of each note. Her eyes dart around the room, looking for expressions of derision among the guests.

Who does she think she is?
Is this a joke?
Oh god...
Isn't she embarrassed?

None of their faces say these things. Molly closes her eyes.

Desmond cannot see the stage from where he is sitting, but by the beginning of the first chorus, he suddenly recognizes the woman he married.

No one is dancing. To Desmond's knowledge, no one has ever danced while Molly sings this song. He moves from his table to the far edge of the stage, where he can watch her in profile.

There is no trace of anxiety in Molly's voice now. Her hands make small shapes in front of her stomach. Desmond can feel his pulse behind his eyes. He takes quick, shallow breaths. On stage, Molly's eyes remain closed.

When the ballad is over, the band moves seamlessly into something more up-tempo, with a syncopated rhythm that makes it impossible for the crowd to stand still. Molly has obviously planned this, and everyone loves her for it.

Now people are dancing. Oh, how they are dancing! And Molly's eyes are still closed, but she is smiling. Her hands make bigger shapes now, up above her head. She should look ridiculous—the mother of the bride playing at being a rock singer—but she is magnificent; she is something different from anyone here. Desmond's palms sweat like a criminal's. A familiar shame grips him. He has stolen a treasure from the world, and dressed her up as a grocer's wife.

Desmond looks to the dance floor, and finds Jonathan singing along to Abby as they dance. Nearby, Suzanne is doing the same to her husband. When they were children, Molly soothed them with this song many times, altering the tempo and melody to accompany Suzanne's first heartbreak; Jonathan's endless sprains, cuts, and bruises. When Desmond was laid off from his job just after Suzanne was born, he and Molly lay in bed together, and Molly held his head to her chest and hummed this tune until he fell asleep. When she quit the band to work—so that Desmond could get his business degree—she chose this as her closing number.

During the bridge, when Desmond returns his boozy gaze to center stage, he finds Molly looking back at him. She nods in time with the music, but her brow is creased. She cocks her head.

Desmond is desperate to apologize, to offer her a chance to reconsider it all—every compromise she has ever made on his behalf. His jaw works behind closed lips. His eyes water; his vision blurs. Molly glows red, and then blue in the rudimentary stage lighting. She disappears for only fractions of seconds as the colored bulbs turn on and off, but for Desmond even these tiny absences are unbearable.

He is starved for absolution. His eyes water and burn. He wants to call out to her... but there is nothing he can say, and the transposition is only a few bars ahead, and he knows that—even at the risk of ruining a perfect performance—Molly will not sing if she thinks that he is upset. So he smiles, and she smiles back. She returns her attention to her audience for the final chorus, and when the song reaches the point where it is supposed to end, instead it goes on.

SITTING BY THE FIRE, 2063 A.D.

I didn't know much about cars back then.

"It smells like burnt popcorn in my car," I told the beautiful mechanic.

She poked her head through the open passenger side window, and sniffed. "Have you been eating popcorn in here?" she asked me.

"Sure. Sometimes," I said.

She looked at me across the roof of the car. "How long do you cook it in the microwave?"

I shrugged. "I don't know. Seven, seven-and-a-half minutes?"

She shook her head. "That's too long."

And that, children, is how I met your grandmother.

LOVE LIFE

THE GENERAL

I was twenty. She was just a little older. She had just moved back to the mainland from Maui. She was my roommate for two days, my girlfriend for six weeks, and then my roommate again for ten months. She shared her surname with a famously ruthless Japanese military leader. I called her The General as a little joke. The second time we slept together she told me to forget the condom; she wanted to feel close to me. If you would have asked me in that moment, I probably would have said I loved her. Nothing came of the lapse, luckily—no infections, and no baby.

A FUN TIME

I met a woman in a bookstore. I talked with her about the author she was browsing. I made reading suggestions. She told me I have a nice voice. (I don't, really. It's thin and reedy, and feminine in embarrassing ways.) Soon we were sharing a dessert at a little restaurant down the street. Next weekend we went to the movies, and she talked loudly throughout. If for no other reason than this, I knew that things wouldn't work out between us. But afterward she still spent the night at my apartment. In the morning, as she was leaving she said "I like your place. I could get used to it here." Next day she texted. Sorry, she wrote. She and her ex had reconciled. Still, she assured me, she had fun.

RHYMING PHRASES

In grade 6, some wonderful trick of fate left me seated to the immediate left of my crush for an entire semester. Our teacher stood in front of the class and insisted on reading a poem I wrote. I kept my head down. I could feel my crush looking at me quizzically as the teacher read. My face burned with a mix of mortification and pride that would become very familiar later in my life.

ACTIVISM

After things between us ran their course, my high school sweetheart and I remained friendly. We lived in the same city after college. She brought me to political events, and introduced me to her activist friends. Sometimes she would get tipsy and try to be my wingman. I struck up a flirtatious conversation with one of the activists. My former-sweetheart observed all of the casual but deliberate touching, and overheard each clumsy innuendo. Later, when I told her that the activist turned down my dinner invitation on account of her longtime boyfriend, my former-sweetheart slurred, "You know what she is? She's a *cock tease*." Thereby forever securing a place in my heart.

SLOW LEARNER

Three pregnancy scares over the course of three years. Each scarier than the last. You'd think that the prospect would have been less frightening as time went on. The fact that it wasn't was a big red flag that I ignored.

DINNER IN

At a party that I almost skipped, I successfully flirted with a smart and beautiful friend of the host. Several weeks later she cooked me dinner in her apartment for my birthday: Chicken breast with caramelized shallots; red potatoes topped with a delicious rosemary and onion concoction; and green beans with lemon. I sat at her dining table and rambled as she cooked. I couldn't think of anything I could do for her that would be as nice as this thing she was doing for me. She wore a snug green t-shirt and gray capri pants. She stood on the balls of her bare feet to check the back burners. I could barely finish a sentence in front of her. For dessert: Braised pears with ginger, topped with vanilla bean ice cream and cinnamon. Blueberry pancakes for breakfast.

CLOGGED DRAINS

"He only wanted me for my hair," she told me, speaking of an old flame. She was fixated on her hair, and assumed everyone else was, too. She lived three hours away, but spent most weekends at my apartment. There were elaborate rituals at night: washing and combing and braiding. I only really noticed her hair when she was gone. There were long curling black strands left in intimate places: Lying on pillow cases. Catching between my toes in the shower. Clinging to whichever of my t-shirts she had made her pajamas. She always joked that it was her way of marking her territory.

MY BIG SOLO

She was an acquaintance—someone pretty that I knew. She was the karaoke DJ at my office's rowdy Christmas party. We made each other laugh. We sang some duets. Infused with a sudden, alien confidence, I decided to ask her on a date. But she beat me to it.

SLANT RHYME

Nineteen years after Grade 6, my crush and I caught up on the last two decades over bottles of red wine on her porch. She rolled little cigarettes by hand. I recounted that day with the poem. We laughed about it. It was dark out, so if my face was burning she couldn't see it.

CONFESSION TIME

Well before all of the chattering at the movies, and our subsequent night together, the girl from the bookstore waved to a table of men in white collars at the restaurant. "That's my priest," she told me.

This is going nowhere fast, I thought.

SHARED GLASS

On our second date—a couple of weeks before the birthday dinner—we took advantage of the unseasonably warm weather and walked to the Herkimer for lunch. The bar was out of the beer she wanted, so our waitress suggested that she wait and taste mine. I made a little joke about the waitress being presumptuous for assuming that we were comfortable drinking from the same glass. As instructed, she tasted my beer when it arrived, and then ordered one of the same for herself. As I prattled on about something or other, she took another drink from my glass—no asking this time, eyes fixed on mine.

Careful... I told myself. I left the waitress an obscenely large tip.

CLOSE CALL

She invited me to her wedding, where she wore her celebrated hair in a dozen intricate braids. During the service her pastor read from the Book of Revelation. At the wedding dinner, her groom asked that everyone stand and recite the Pledge of Allegiance. I laughed with my date about how I had dodged a bullet. Then I went home with her, and spent the next three years with her, getting sick again and again at the thought of those pregnancy tests coming back positive.

EXIT STRATEGY

A month into our courtship, the General began receiving mail from a California prison. I looked the other way at first, but eventually we had a talk, and she came clean. She was engaged to a cocaine smuggler. He had told her he was an air conditioning repairman at first. She was upset with him when he was arrested, but had decided to stand by her man—at least until his sentencing hearing. I said that I understood, and then shut myself in my bedroom across the hall for the next ten months.

LAST CHANCE FOR A SLOW DANCE

We realized at prom that neither of us had many friends. My high school sweetheart and I swayed back and forth in that awkward teenage two-step. I felt stupid and self-conscious for being there at all. Things have to get better than this, I thought.

As we danced, my high school sweetheart locked her knees and began rocking in place, moaning like a zombie. Thereby forever securing a place in my heart.

DUET

I don't even feel all that sick, but she tells me that she doesn't like the sound of my cough, and that my face is flushed. She tells me that if this fever—slight as it is—doesn't break by morning, then I'm not going to work. I grumble something back and we go to bed. Sometime before the sun is up, I feel her palm cupping my forehead. My skin is cool now. My pillowcase is damp, but drying. Her hand slips away and we fall back to sleep without a word. But when morning comes, the memory of her warm, dry palm remains, and I silently repeat the promise, over and over:

For the rest of my life, I will try to deserve this...
For the rest of my life, I will try to deserve this...
For the rest of my life, I will try to deserve this...
For the rest of my life, I will try to deserve this...

THANK YOU

Kiel Mutschelknaus. For lending his considerable talents to the design of this book, and for obliging my (unrelated) requests for grotesque drawings of serial murderer cartoon bears.

Joe Thoen. For lending his name to the protagonist of "You Gotta Have a Hook," and for being an all around great pal.

Christopher Monks, John Warner, and the good folks at McSweeney's. For giving my work its first audience outside of a classroom.

The South Dakota Arts Council. For generously supporting what many would consider a questionable endeavor.

The Get Fresh Crew at Fresh Produce. For inviting me in, and making me uncomfortable.

John Boylan. For the title inspiration.

Caitlin Pisha. For the layout consultation.

Patricia Hampl. For the early, enthusiastic support.

Thomas Haley. For the reading lists.

Mary Winstead. For telling me I could do better.

Charles Baxter. For the career advice. It's true: loan processing is no way for a writer to pay the bills.

Ted Heeren. For the daily reminders that there are no rules.

Matt Staab. My first publisher.

The "My DJ" video production crew: Joe Hubers, Wes Eisenhauer, Corey Gerlach, Andrew Reinartz, Lucy Albers, and everyone who showed up to make disapproving faces at me on camera. For turning a goofy little story into a goofy little movie.

Darryl Gudmundson, Brad Schulz, and the folks at *Funny or Die*. For voting "Funny."

Maggie Wander and Emily Casey. For honesty that has made me a better writer, and for friendship that has made me a better person.

Brienne Maner. For making me laugh every day. For keeping me home when I'm sick. For letting me make up the harmonies. For today. For tomorrow.

PUBLICATION HISTORY

These originally appeared on *McSweeney's Internet Tendency:*
   "Tales of Erotica: Chuck Norris & Me"
   "My DJ"
   "What Kind of Ghost Do You Have?"
   "I'm Not Here to Hold Your Hand;
      I'm Here to Run a Business"

Versions of these appeared on *ThePostSD:*
   "How I Would Fight Certain Animals"
   "Please Help Me Find My Backpack"
   "The Year in Film: 1976"

Versions of these appeared on *The Ghosts & Horses Radio Hour* podcast:
   "Love Life"
   "How to Not Lie at the Blood Bank"
   "Sitting by the Fire, 2063 A.D."
   "Doctors"
   "Amphetamine Twice Monthly"
   "Violent Acts in Appropriate Settings"

"Tales of Erotica: Chuck Norris & Me" also appeared in *McSweeney's Joke Book of Book Jokes* (Vintage, 2008).

INDEX

ABOUT THE AUTHOR

Brian Bieber lives in Sioux Falls, South Dakota. He is the writer and producer of *The Ghosts & Horses Radio Hour*.

Photo by Brienne Maner

GhostsAndHorses.com